The Adventures of
Guh the Wonderdog
Guh Meets His Family

by Brittney Hall

DORRANCE
PUBLISHING CO
EST. 1920
PITTSBURGH, PENNSYLVANIA 15238

Dorrance Publishing Co
585 Alpha Drive
Suite 103
Pittsburgh, PA 15238
Visit our website at www.dorrancebookstore.com

ISBN: 978-1-4809-3216-6
eISBN: 978-1-4809-3193-0

The Adventures of
Guh the Wonderdog
Guh Meets His Family

One cold spring day,

Mommy and Daddy

took their little girl on a drive.

They did not tell the little girl

where they were going,

so she patiently waited

and stared out the car window,

trying to figure out

what her parents were up to.

Finally, they arrived in a neighborhood

and pulled up to a brown house.

This looked like any other house,

except behind the fence

there were eleven black and white puppies

running around playing.

The puppies were waiting

to go to their forever homes.

Mommy and Daddy told the little girl

that one of these puppies

was going home with them!

From that moment on,

their life would never be the same.

They were taking home a wonderdog!

The family named the puppy George.

The little girl decided that George

was too difficult to say,

so instead, she called him 'Guh'.

Guh was born with the identity

of something great,

something rare.

He was a wonderdog!

Although he was small,

he knew he was bound for greatness.

Now that he had a family of people

to please and protect,

he was not going to let them down!

Guh loved his family.

He loved them so much

that he wanted to be with them

all the time.

He never wanted to sleep in his crate,

so instead he pleaded his case

with barks and whines

until his little girl pulled him up

onto her bed to sleep.

She was surprised how much room

a little puppy could take up!

The pup could not wait

for the sun to come up

and get his day started;

there were too many things

to explore in his new home.

He would wake up at 5:00 a.m.

ready for action.

Then, as puppies do, he would get tired

and would take a morning nap at 7:00 a.m.

while Mommy made breakfast.

Mommy was not sure this puppy

was such a good idea after all.

It felt like now she had two kids,

but she could see how her little girl

and the puppy adored each other.

A pair of best friends had just been made.

She could see that Guh

and the little girl

had many adventures ahead of them.

CPSIA information can be obtained
at www.ICGtesting.com
Printed in the USA
LVOW05*0102080317
526486LV00043B/1128/P